FIDDLER
AND HIS
BROTHERS

TORD NYGREN

FIDDLER
AND HIS
BROTHERS
TORD NYGREN

WILLIAM MORROW AND CO., INC.
New York

A woodcutter and his wife once lived in a cabin at the foot of a high mountain. As the years passed, they had three sons. The first grew to be as strong as a bear, so he was called Teddy. The second grew to be as fast as a horse, so he was called Neddy. The third son was neither very strong nor very fast, but he could play the violin like an angel. Folks called him Fiddler.

People were always calling out to him, "Fiddler, play us a tune." Then they would dance or sing along, forgetting for a while the cares of the day. Fiddler grew to be a most popular young man, while his brothers grew jealous of him and his fiddle.

The day came when the three brothers were sent out into the world to seek their fortunes. "You may come along with us," said Teddy and Neddy to Fiddler, "only if you promise not to play that blasted fiddle of yours."

"I'll play only when you ask me to," said Fiddler.

"Not much chance of that," sneered his brothers.

The brothers went from farm to farm seeking work. No one seemed to need a young man with the strength of a bear or one with the speed of a horse. Often though, the farmer would call out, "You there with the fiddle! Give us a tune and you boys can have a bite to eat before you go on your way."

So Teddy and Neddy were forced to ask Fiddler to please get out his fiddle and play. The three would get their meal all right, but Fiddler would get no thanks from his brothers. In fact, they liked him even less.

Late one evening, the brothers arrived at the edge of a lake. In the center of the lake they could see an island, and in the center of the island, a brilliant light. Where there is light there must be people, thought the boys, so they found a small boat and rowed out to the island.

As they walked toward the light, they saw an old woman wearing a beautiful vest embroidered all over with roses. She was sweeping outside a little house while a younger woman held up a lantern that turned night into day. The women had a billy goat with long golden horns. From these horns hung little golden bells that tinkled with the most beautiful music. As the boys watched from behind some trees, the two women took the goat and the lantern and went into the house.

The brothers wondered if they should knock at the door and ask for a night's shelter. "I think they look like witches," said Teddy.

Since it was so late, the brothers plucked up their courage, knocked at the door, and went in. The two women were standing by the hearth, cooking porridge. They had such evil, piercing eyes that it was obvious at once that they were witches indeed—mother and daughter.

Fiddler stepped forward. "My name's Fiddler, and these are my brothers, Teddy and Neddy," he said. "We were wondering if we might sleep here tonight."

"No, you may not," shouted the witch's daughter. "Now get out!" Teddy and Neddy fled at once, but Fiddler, who was not easily frightened, stayed where he was.

"Where did you get that fine embroidered vest, old woman?" Fiddler asked.

"None of your business," answered the witch.

"And where did you get the goat with the golden horns?" Fiddler asked.

"I take what I want," said the witch, "and you're so nosy that I'm going to take you and your fiddle as well. You won't get away from here alive."

"You may take many things," said Fiddler, "but not me." In a flash, he was out the door. He ran to his brothers and they rowed out on the dark lake, away from the witches' island.

They rowed to the other side of the lake and spent the night there under a tree. When they awoke, they could see a great mansion in the distance, surrounded by fields and meadows. They walked toward it, hoping to find work.

In a garden behind a blue gate, they saw a man, a woman, and a young girl walking among the flowers. The girl was as beautiful and as sweet as wild strawberries. She smiled so prettily at the boys that they forgot to introduce themselves.

"Good morning," said the man to the three brothers. "I am the king of this land, and this is the queen, and this is our daughter, Princess Ingrid. How may I be of service to you?"

Teddy, Neddy, and Fiddler bowed low and asked if there might be any work for them on the king's lands.

"What can you do?" asked the king.

"I'm as strong as a bear," said Teddy.

"Then you may work at the mill," said the king.

"I'm as fast as a horse," said Neddy.

"Then you may work in the stables," replied the king.

"I can do nothing but play the fiddle," said the youngest brother.

"I love music," said the king. "You may be my court musician."

So all the brothers went into the king's service, and one job was as good as another, but Teddy and Neddy were still jealous of Fiddler and wished they could be rid of him.

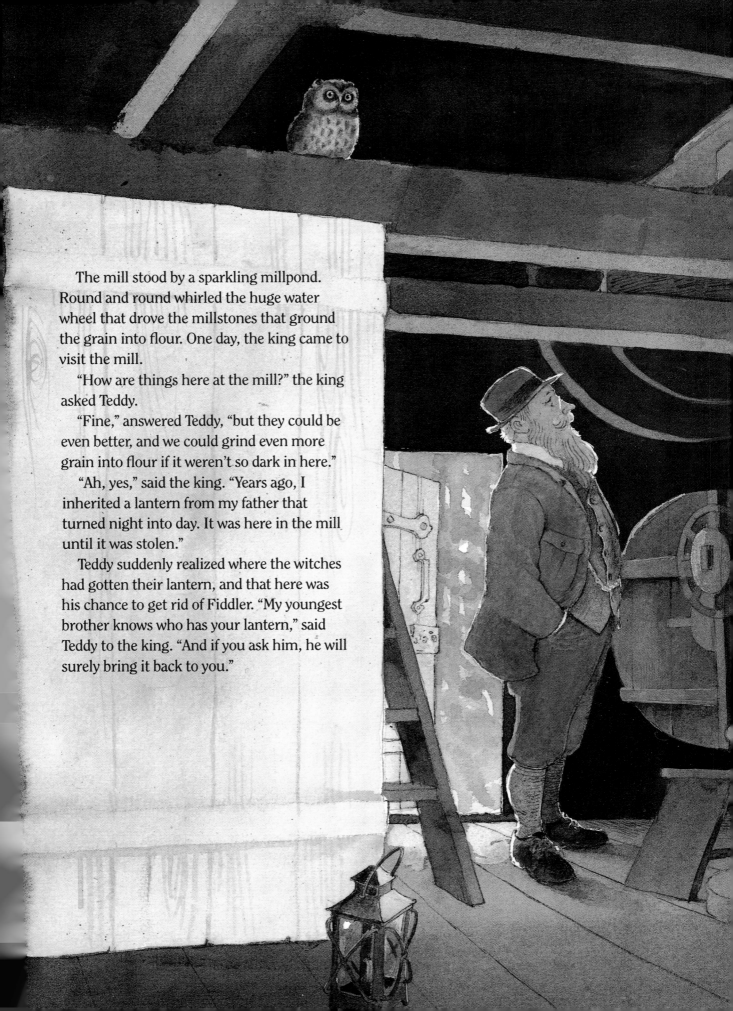

The mill stood by a sparkling millpond. Round and round whirled the huge water wheel that drove the millstones that ground the grain into flour. One day, the king came to visit the mill.

"How are things here at the mill?" the king asked Teddy.

"Fine," answered Teddy, "but they could be even better, and we could grind even more grain into flour if it weren't so dark in here."

"Ah, yes," said the king. "Years ago, I inherited a lantern from my father that turned night into day. It was here in the mill until it was stolen."

Teddy suddenly realized where the witches had gotten their lantern, and that here was his chance to get rid of Fiddler. "My youngest brother knows who has your lantern," said Teddy to the king. "And if you ask him, he will surely bring it back to you."

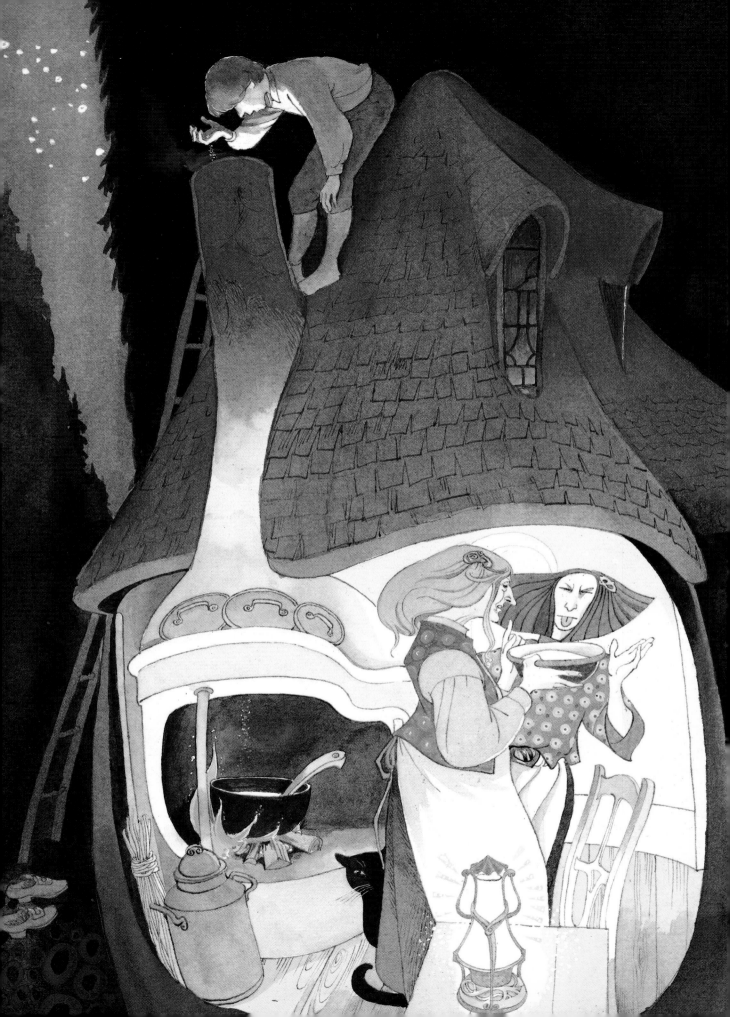

The king went to Fiddler and said, "If you can bring back the lantern that turns night into day, you shall have both fields and meadows."

Fiddler thought that would be a fine reward for the lantern. He put a bag of salt into his pocket and, when evening came, rowed out to the witches' island.

As quiet as a mouse, he crept up to the house. The door was open, and by the light of the stolen lantern, Fiddler could see the witch and her daughter cooking their porridge. Fiddler climbed up onto the roof of the house. He pulled out his bag of salt and poured some down the chimney, straight into the porridge.

The witch could not understand how the porridge could be so salty. She decided to cook some fresh porridge and sent her daughter to the spring to fetch some water. The witch's daughter took the lantern and a bucket and went through the forest to the spring. She did not notice Fiddler following her.

When the witch's daughter arrived at the spring, she put down the lantern and bent over to fill her bucket. Fiddler, who had been hiding behind a tree, crept up and gave her a push. With a great splash she fell headlong into the cold, murky water.

Fiddler grabbed the lantern and raced through the forest back to his boat. As he began to row, he could hear the witch's daughter's dreadful howling as she stumbled through the dark forest, angry and sodden.

The witch, too, heard the din. As quickly as she could, she ran to the shore. Far out on the lake shone the lantern that turned night into day.

"Is that you, Fiddler?" called the witch.

"None other, old woman," said Fiddler.

"Have you taken my lantern?" asked the witch.

"I have indeed," Fiddler responded.

"And how did you take it without our seeing you?" she called.

"Perhaps someday I'll tell you," answered Fiddler.

When Fiddler returned to the king's house, there was great rejoicing, and the king gave Fiddler both fields and meadows as he had promised.

In the stables where Neddy worked, there was an empty stall, above which hung a golden bell. One day, the king and Princess Ingrid came to visit the stables.

"How is the work going?" asked the king.

"Fine, thank you," said Neddy, "but I've been wondering who is going to live in the empty stall."

The king told Neddy about the wonderful billy goat that had been given to Princess Ingrid as a birthday present by her godmother. The goat had golden horns hung with little golden bells, and anyone who heard them ring could not be unhappy. The goat had been Princess Ingrid's dearest playmate until someone had stolen it one night.

Neddy knew that this must be the goat he had seen at the witches' house. "My younger brother knows where your goat can be found," said Neddy to the king. "If you ask him, he will surely bring it back to you."

"Now we'll be rid of Fiddler for sure," Neddy said to himself. "He'll never be able to take the goat without the witches hearing him."

The king went to Fiddler and said, "If you bring back our golden goat, you shall have a magnificent house to live in."

"That's a fine reward for a goat," said Fiddler, and out he rowed to the witches' island. This time, too, it was night when he arrived. He crept up to the witches' house just as the witch's daughter was about to lock up for the night. Fiddler slipped a branch between the door and the doorpost so that the door would not lock.

"Leave the door open," said the witch, "and we'll see what's wrong tomorrow when it's light." Without the king's lantern, it was now dark in their house at night.

When the witches were asleep, Fiddler stole into the house. The golden-horned goat was asleep in front of the hearth, and Fiddler quickly stuffed cotton wool into all the bells so that their ringing would not awaken the witches.

With the golden goat in his arms, Fiddler ran to his boat and rowed out onto the lake. Then he took the cotton out of the bells, and at once the most beautiful music filled the air. The witches woke up and hurried to the shore.

"Is that you, Fiddler?" called the witch.

"It certainly is, old woman," said Fiddler.

"Have you taken our golden goat?" said the witch.

"I certainly have," said Fiddler.

"And how did you do it without our hearing you?" asked the witch.

"Perhaps someday I'll tell you," answered Fiddler.

While the witches whined and wailed on the shore, Fiddler rowed back to the king's house.

Everyone was overjoyed when Fiddler returned with the golden goat. Princess Ingrid hugged both Fiddler and the goat. The king had the finest timber cut down in the forest, and a magnificent house was built for Fiddler. So now he had fields and meadows and a house. The only ones who were not happy to see Fiddler again were his brothers.

One Sunday after Fiddler had played for the royal family, the queen said, "Fiddler, you have brought us back our lantern and our golden goat. Perhaps you might also find the rose vest my mother gave me when I was a young girl. When one wears it, one is never ill." Fiddler knew this must be the same vest the old witch wore.

"If you can fetch the queen's vest," said the king, "you shall have Princess Ingrid as your wife. We have noticed that you are very fond of each other."

"That's a fine reward indeed for a vest," said Fiddler, "and of course I want Ingrid if she will have me."

Teddy and Neddy had been standing outside, listening. How happy they were! Now they would be rid of Fiddler once and for all. He would never be able to take the vest from the witch.

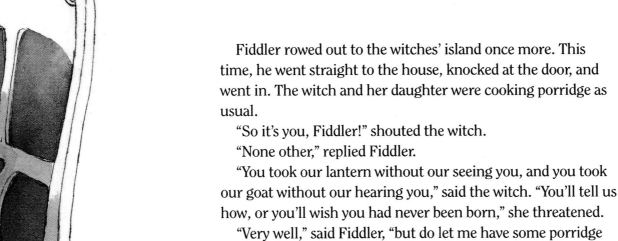

Fiddler rowed out to the witches' island once more. This time, he went straight to the house, knocked at the door, and went in. The witch and her daughter were cooking porridge as usual.

"So it's you, Fiddler!" shouted the witch.

"None other," replied Fiddler.

"You took our lantern without our seeing you, and you took our goat without our hearing you," said the witch. "You'll tell us how, or you'll wish you had never been born," she threatened.

"Very well," said Fiddler, "but do let me have some porridge while I explain." The witch's daughter gave him a bowl, and he began to speak.

"You see, old woman," he began, "this jacket I'm wearing is no ordinary jacket. Whoever wears it has only to give each button a twist and a turn, and then no one can see him or hear him. That way, he can take whatever he wishes and no one's the wiser."

The greedy old witch thought of all she might steal if she had Fiddler's jacket. "You'll give me that jacket or you won't leave here alive," she snarled at Fiddler. Fiddler, pretending to be frightened, quickly removed his jacket and handed it to the witch.

The witch removed her rose vest, and as her daughter helped her put on Fiddler's jacket, Fiddler picked up the witch's vest and slipped quietly out the door. When he was halfway across the lake, he heard the witch shouting at him from the shore.

"Fiddler, it's not working! Tell me which way to twist and which way to turn."

"You can twist and turn every which way for all the good it will do you," answered Fiddler. "That jacket's no more magic than a bowl of porridge."

Fiddler could hear the witches ranting and raving as he rowed on toward the king's house and his new bride.

After they were married, Fiddler and Princess Ingrid moved into their new house. The wheat grew tall in their fields, and the cows grazed happily in their meadows. The golden goat dined on the juiciest clover and the greenest grass. The sound of its bells could be heard far and wide, making everyone happy. The sound reached even the mill and the stables, and no one who is happy can be either wicked or jealous.

Except perhaps for witches.

First published in Sweden in 1986
under the title SPELEVINK OCH HANS BRODER
by Bokförlaget Opal AB,
Stockholm, Sweden.
Inquiries should be addressed to William Morrow and Company, Inc.,
105 Madison Avenue,
New York, NY 10016.

Printed in the United States of America.
1 2 3 4 5 6 7 8 9 10

Library of Congress Cataloging-in-Publication Data
Nygren, Tord, 1936-
Fiddler and his brothers.
Translation of: Spelevink och hans bröder.
Summary: Three brothers go off to seek their
fortunes, but the one who plays the fiddle, having
the most wit and courage, comes off best.
[1. Fairy tales] I. Title.
PZ8.N982Fi 1987 [E]   86-31297
ISBN 0-688-07145-7
ISBN 0-688-07146-5 (lib. bdg.)